with a kiss upon
your brow.

So fall asleep, my angel . . .

But there comes a time for sleeping,
and our sleepy time is now.

I could hold your hand in my hand as I sit beside your bed.

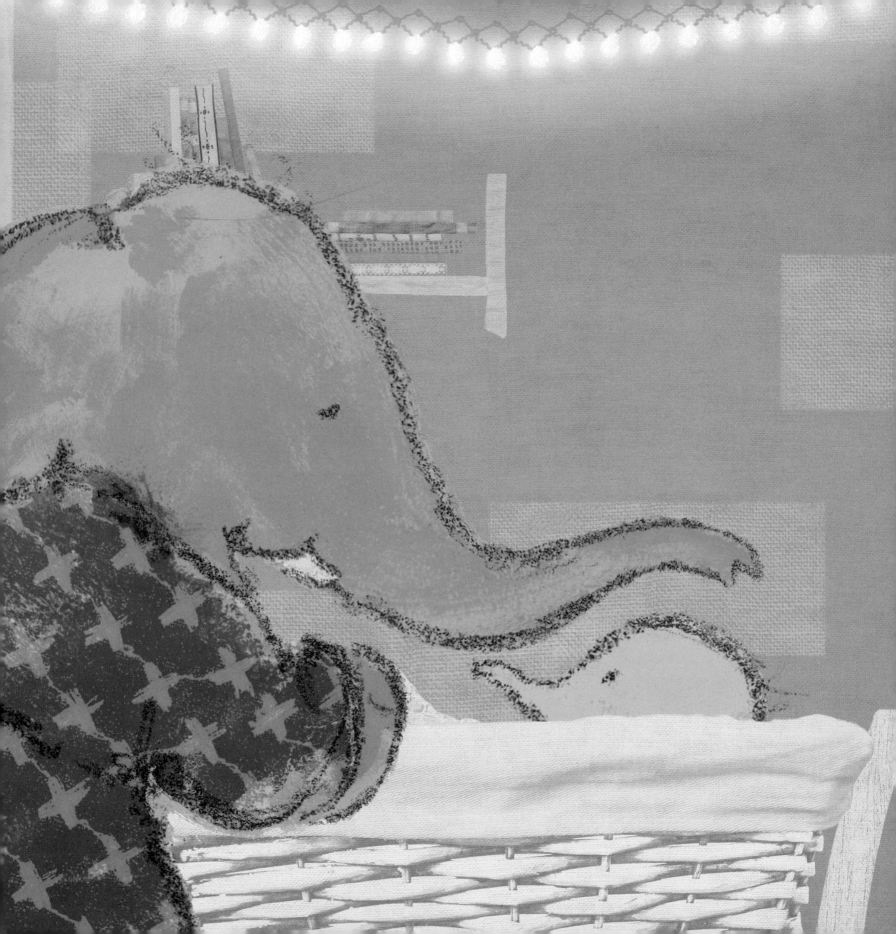

I could pat your
precious head.

I could listen to you breathing.

I could sing you all the songs
that my mother sang to me.

I could sit you on my knee.

I could stroke your silky hair.

I could whisper lots of stories
till the darkness turns to light.

I could gaze at you all night.

I could rock you in my arms.

I could gobble up your toes.

I could munch your tiny fingers.

I could nibble on your nose.

I could eat your little ears.

For Dr. Linda McKendrick and Dr. Sanjay Sinhal,
with thanks for Theo—M. F.

For Guy—E. Q.

E
Fox,
Mem

BEACH LANE BOOKS • An imprint of Simon & Schuster Children's Publishing Division •1230 Avenue of the Americas, New York, New York 10020 • Text copyright © 2013 by Mem Fox • Illustrations copyright © 2013 by Emma Quay • First published in 2013 by Penguin Australia/Viking • First U.S. edition 2014 • All rights reserved, including the right of reproduction in whole or in part in any form. • BEACH LANE BOOKS is a trademark of Simon & Schuster, Inc. • For information about special discounts for bulk purchases, please contact Simon & Schuster Special Sales at 1-866-506-1949 or business@simonandschuster.com. • The Simon & Schuster Speakers Bureau can bring authors to your live event. For more information or to book an event, contact the Simon & Schuster Speakers Bureau at 1-866-248-3049 or visit our website at www.simonspeakers.com. • Book design by Lauren Rille • The text for this book is set in Amasis. • The illustrations for this book were created using pencil, acrylic paints, and Photoshop. The patterns and textures are from knitting and objects found in charity shops, including handkerchiefs, doilies, lace, belts, and baskets. • Manufactured in the United States of America • 0514 PCR • 10 9 8 7 6 5 4 3 2 1 • Library of Congress Cataloging-in-Publication Data • Fox, Mem, 1946– • Baby bedtime / Mem Fox, Emma Quay.—First US edition. • p. cm. • "Originally published in 2013 by Penguin Australia/Viking"—Copyright page. • Summary: "After all the kissing and the hugging and the rocking and the snuggling, there at last comes a time for sleeping"—Provided by publisher. • ISBN 978-1-4814-2097-6 (hardcover) • ISBN 978-1-4814-2098-3 (eBook) • [1. Stories in rhyme. 2. Bedtime—Fiction. 3. Babies—Fiction. 4. Lullabies.] I. Quay, Emma, illustrator. II. Title. • PZ8.3.F8245Bab 2014 • [E]—dc23 • 2013045559

Baby Bedtime

Mem Fox

illustrated by
Emma Quay

Beach Lane Books ★ New York London Toronto Sydney New Delhi